Fangs 'n' Fire

Ten Dramatic Dragon tales

adapted, written and illustrated by

Chris Mould

h
Hodder
Children's
Books

A division of Hachette Children's Books

Don't search too hard for the Dragon!

However hard you look,

he will only appear when he wants to.

But once in a while, he may pass your way. Don't expect the ferocious beast you've heard of. He may be still and silent, or appear unnoticed in clouds of smoke or flames of fire. Perhaps he's small and scuttles, rat-like, out of sight before you spot him.

Who knows? Listen to my tales of this creature and maybe then you'll know him better.

Contents

A Twist in the Tale

By Chris Mould

The light from the village campfire flickered dancing shadows across Edgar's frightened face as his father told him of the old Nordic Dragon. Somewhere out there on the cliff top, where the icy blow of the north-west wind sent the grass reeling in circles and the crash of the sea echoed around the rocks, he lay in wait. With his great curled horns and fiery yellow eyes he was known to greet any contender to his cliff-top throne with a stare that would loosen their grip on the cliff face.

And that alone would be enough to send anyone brave enough to try it, plunging back into the sea. So many had tried to complete the task, and failed, that it became a worthy challenge. A challenge that young Edgar must now undertake to prove to the people that he was worthy of the sword and shield that had been given to him.

Poor Edgar. His father was a notable warrior, a doer of great deeds, and to follow in his footsteps was proving a tough task. Too much expectation had been placed on him already. He was a mere stripling of a lad and he would struggle just to lift the blade that lay at his side.

The firelight flickered and finally Edgar's eyelids grew tired and heavy. Under the fading glow of the embers he slept and dreamed of the old dragon. It appeared to him in many forms. At first it grew out from the flames of the fire and bellowed huge flames into the air. Then he watched it mould its shape in the sparking smoke that bubbled upwards into the dark blue sky, mingling with the clouds.

All night he battled with it in his dreams. He saw the great horns and burning eyes as clearly as if they were right there in front of him. And when he woke he was determined to complete his task.

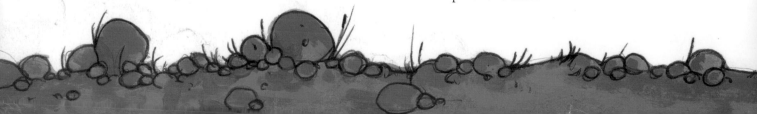

Soon the word had spread. Young Edgar was about to face the challenge. He gritted his teeth, swallowed the nervous lump in his throat and made his way. Not only was Edgar no warrior, he was no oarsman either. He struggled to take his boat the short distance out to sea where the needle-like cliff soared up through the breaking surf. No sooner had he got going than he began doubting his capabilities. He looked back at the shore where the villagers stood in wait. The fire still burned around them and, as he ventured further from them, the dancing yellow flames were all that he could see.

Before too long he had made it to the cliff face and he clambered out of his vessel, tying it to a suitable rocky post. His knees knocked and he stumbled awkwardly across the slippery surface of the boulders that spilled around the bottom of the climb.

He grabbed his trusty sword and stared hard at its sharpened edge to compose himself. In truth his blade had only ever cut its way through the dense undergrowth in the woodlands but he hoped that he was about to change his reputation. With the sword tucked into the garments that were tied across his back he stared up at the towering rock and made his way.

It was hard and craggy and a biting wind gnawed at his face but he knew he must carry on. He peered down as he secured his feet into the crevices of the slippery stone and pushed upward. He had sworn he would not look, but he could not resist a glance across to the shore where the crowd appeared like a small group of ants as they watched him move upwards.

His hands bled and his fingers froze but still he pushed on. He thought that by now he might hear the roar of the great dragon or perhaps he would hear the beating of its wings. And he wondered if it might leave its perch and attack him as he clung on helplessly to the cliff face.

All these things raced through his mind and sent his head spinning but he held his composure as he neared the top. Now the day grew dark and he readied himself, constantly checking that he could quickly reach his blade over his shoulder if he needed to.

At length he had almost reached the top and his nervousness felt like it might overwhelm him completely as he prepared to poke his head over the edge. But before he could get so far the beast made the first move.

In a sudden darting movement the curling great horns of the beast appeared, followed by two ghastly yellow eyes with strangely formed pupils of a peculiar shape. A snorting of breath came with it and the great grey beard he had heard of dangled over the edge and was so close to him that it touched his face.

Through the darkness the surprised whites of Edgar's eyes shone like stars and in a moment of sheer panic at the ghastly vision, he lost his grip. He had made a vain attempt to reach for his sword, but in doing so, he completely lost his hold on the cliff face. He fell headlong and backward towards the rolling surf below.

His body speared down into the deep and a thousand tiny bubbles circled around him in the dark. He would have disappeared completely had it not been for a small boat of returning fishermen who pulled his pathetic figure out from the water like a drowned rat.

The next morning he awoke in his bed with his mother at his side. She put a drink up to his lips and stared into his weary eyes.

'He's awake Erik!' she called out and the formidable shape of his father wandered into the room, peering down at him, half smiling at his shivering, worn-out figure.

'Perhaps it will take a little longer to make a warrior out of you, Edgar!' his father chuckled, and then that was all he remembered before he drifted back to sleep.

And just a short distance away from where Edgar lay in his bed the sun shone down on the flattened grassy top of the cliff, and as it did so it warmed the gnarled old face of a mountain goat that chewed away at the greenery. He brushed his curled horns against a gorse bush and stared down at the sea through his yellowy eyes. And then, preening and scratching his great grey beard on a nearby branch, he carried on eating and wondered when he would next see another face appear up over the parapet.

George and the Dragon

Traditional Tale

Long ago, in the city of Silene, the seeds of dragon lore and legend were sown. This is how it began. A young man was peering out of the window of a tower. He was in no hurry to go back to his tasks and he leant forward on the sill with his face resting in one hand, catching the afternoon sun with his eyes half shut. But something begged him to turn and look: a noise of some kind, a disturbance nearby, a great heaving and grumbling and shifting of something big and ungodly.

You would have laughed if you had seen the young man's expression. It went from dozy and only half interested to alert and frightened in disbelief. He rubbed his eyes and looked again. 'Too much sun,' he said, looking at the sky accusingly. But no he was right. It really was there, beside the well, not far from the city's gates.

He thundered down the stone steps into the heart of the temple and shouted out loud to all who could hear that they must come quickly and see what the devil had delivered to the people of Silene.

And the people came running, not believing his cries, but curious all the same. They had to see what was making him cause such a fuss. The King of Silene cursed him for disturbing his rest but he too came to look, picking up the hem of his robe so that he might not trip as he rushed along.

They all stood outside the gates and gazed into the shimmering heat on the horizon. Something had wrapped itself around the old tree.

It was a huge, crusty old dragon, curled up around the tree's gnarled old trunk, looking like it had been baked in the sun for far too long.

It was a curious red colour and a small pair of wings sprang out from its shoulders. It lay slumped, half across the dusty road and half over the well, the only water supply for many miles.

It was likely that none of them had ever seen a dragon before and even more likely that none of them would know what to do. And none of them did. But it was a problem and it needed solving.

The king pondered over this for some time. And so did his advisors and the villagers and the farmers and anyone who was anything to do with Silene. But no one had a solution. It was decided eventually that they should sit together in the great hall and stay there until an answer was found. So the people assembled and waited for the arrival of their king.

Shortly, he entered. Wherever he went his daughter was at his side and today was no exception. He was a proud man and when he looked on her he saw the future queen of Silene. Her mother would have been so proud to see her grow into someone so beautiful.

The whole city now sat in discussion. They talked all day. When the light grew dim the candles were lit and still they talked.

Now it was one problem that the people could not reach the water, but another, that after he had rested there a while, the old dragon grew hungry. It wouldn't be long before he went looking for a meal. And the city was too close for comfort.

When the king had sat in discussion with the people of Silene for what seemed like for ever they came to an agreement. They would feed a sheep to the dragon whenever he grew restless. In that way, they would avoid a confrontation with him for he was a fearsome-looking beast. The sun shone on the scales of his back and his nostrils smouldered in warning of the fearsome fire that rested deep inside him. They were sure that he was better off left alone.

The arrangement worked well. When the dragon had eaten his fill, he would sleep for the rest of the day and the villagers would come and take the water from the well as he dozed.

But this uneasy truce wouldn't last for ever.

'Look,' said the farmers. 'Where shall we be without our sheep? Soon there will be no more. Then what will we do?' They had to find a way; they didn't dare mess with the might of the beast.

And though it seemed like the worst possible solution the answer lay with the very people of Silene. Each night all the names of the people were placed in a huge pot and then one name was taken from inside it. The following morning that person would be sacrificed to the dragon. No one liked

the idea but that was the way it was going to be.

Soon the word spread outside the city that a dragon plagued the land. Before long brave knights would appear at the gates and promise the king that they would rid Silene of its troubles.

So the king filled a huge trough with riches. Whoever slew the great dragon would take the prize and the people would live in peace. The pot of shining gold tempted many a brave warrior. But no man was good enough.

Many came and all of them failed: some were burned by the blistering fire from the dragon's throat; others were sliced in two by its razor-sharp teeth; three were ripped apart by its huge claws and one was even whipped with its tail.

All of them perished and the pot of money stayed where it was, gathering dust and cobwebs, and the villagers carried on dwindling in their numbers.

It was not long before the King of Silene was struck with a nasty surprise. His daughter's name was pulled out from the pot one night and he was stricken with grief. He begged the people not to take her and he promised them every ounce of treasure in the whole kingdom if they would guarantee her safety. But it was not to be. At the insistence of the villagers the king was forced to endure the same circumstances as his people and his daughter was handed over to the dragon.

But as the king's daughter was escorted towards the dragon's lair a bold young knight headed along the road into Silene. He had heard of the beast that terrorized the city and devoured many brave warriors.

When he arrived he was struck by the sheer size of the beast but he insisted that the king's daughter should return to her father.

'Go and tell your king that George is here and promise him that the dragon that dwells outside his walls will not live until sunset.'

Right there and then a fearsome fight ensued.

A crowd had gathered but stayed well back, near a small outcrop of trees where they could watch from the safety of the lofty branches.

As the knight approached on his horse flames billowed from the mouth of the dragon and the horse reared up on its hind legs. The knight thrust his lance into the belly of the beast but its scales were tough and leathery and they would not give. The limbs and wings of the beast flapped and clashed with the shield of the warrior. Again George thrust his lance into its side but this time it shattered into a thousand pieces and he fell from his horse, hard on the ground. A huge claw landed inches from his side, striking the breastplate of his armour.

He pulled out his sword from his side and swung it wildly this way and that. Each time he missed. The dragon's swift movements belied its hulking great frame. It bobbed and weaved and tested the skill of the warrior.

But at great length George's movements were quicker. He climbed up on to the base of its neck so that the dragon's teeth could not reach him and then he sank his blade into its shoulders. He watched its blood run red over the scales that formed its skin and then he felt it start to wilt

as it dropped motionless to the dry earth.

Where great flames had leapt from its gaping mouth its tongue now hung out through a gap in its teeth and a puff of blackened smoke announced that the fire inside had burned out.

A roar of cheers filled the air and, having come out to join his people, the king, addressed the hero.

'You have saved my daughter and you have saved my kingdom. You must have heard of the riches that lay in wait for the brave knight who would rid Silene of the dragon. Come back to our city and take the reward that belongs to you.'

But George wanted nothing.

'Give me food for the night and a warm bed and tomorrow I will be on my way. Then I will take to the road and do good somewhere else.'

And in the morning the people of Silene watched George climb back up on to his horse and disappear into the sun. From that day on he was known as Saint George, who did something for others without wanting anything in return, and wherever he went people would know his name.

Dragonesque

By Chris Mould

I was never sure about Mister Tallis.

Right from the beginning I always felt there was something unusual about him. With his tall dark shape, his cold, unusual manner and his tell-tale eyes.

It was Christmas Eve and bitterly cold. Crisp white snow had fallen all afternoon and hidden the uneven surface made by the cobbles. The light faded and it grew late. Gathering drifts piled up in the doorways of the houses and the gas lamps glowed like fireflies in the dark. Inside it was warm and peaceful.

I heard a crunching of snow and a long, willowy shadow passed the window before a knock sounded upon the door.

'Could you tell your father that Mister Tallis is here,' instructed the tall, dark figure. It was the first time he had called, but after this, he always came.

I did not know what business he had with my father. I would be sent upstairs and they would sit together by the fireside, talking in whispers. I always felt my father seemed unnerved by him as I watched sneakily through the balustrades at the top of the steps. He seemed to perch on the edge of his seat while Mister Tallis sat easily in the wing-backed chair with his hands poised in front of him.

I never caught their conversation but I remained convinced that he had some hold over my father. There was always an exchange of money before he left with my father scratching around in his wallet for gold coins.

But one particular night I noticed something that convinced me that
Mister Tallis was even more unusual than I had first thought. He sat in
the same piece of furniture as he had always done but it was later than
usual and the light was different. And then I noticed it as I stared
through the gaps at the top of the stairs.

It was his shadow.

It was somehow the wrong shape. The shape, perhaps, of something else. It was tall and elongated, as he was, but it seemed to take on the unlikely form of something beastly. It was almost dragonesque!

It was then that I began to take a closer interest in Mister Tallis. Soon I noticed that he visited the other houses also. Come rain or shine he would be at their doors. I was sure that he took money from all the people in the village and I was determined to find out why. My father said it was just 'business' and refused to discuss it any further.

However much I tried I could get no one to speak of the man they called Mister Tallis. Everyone changed the subject. One day, I was walking back through the village and I passed some young children playing in the grounds of the park. 'The dragon man is coming,' they screamed as they ran to hide. But when I asked, no one knew who the dragon man was. Did they speak of whom I suspected?

Late one night I watched him. My intention was to follow him home. The snow still lay upon the ground and no one was out. No one except, of course, for the man himself, in his long dark coat and his wide-brimmed hat, carrying a case and winding through the streets with his sinuous stride. I watched him until he had disappeared out of sight and then I could not stop myself from stealing out into the night to discover where he went.

I can only try and describe what happened next. It seems impossible that it could happen but yet at the same time, I was sure that it did. I followed Mister Tallis at a safe distance. I stopped at the corners and poked my head around slowly each time to be sure that he would not see me. His lofty, dark shape walked on ahead. And then as he came to the outside of the village I swear his form began to change. He was a silhouette by now and only the moon lit the way as it played upon the carpet of snow ahead.

But somehow, the silhouette began to transform as he walked. He never stopped; he just kept on walking. The shape of his coat tails fluttered in the breeze but as they flapped and swirled they became huge bat-like wings at his back. Then somehow he morphed perfectly and smoothly from his two legged gait into a four-legged stoop. Then a long and slender deadly whip of a tail slithered snake-like at his back. He went from slow to quick to lightning speed and then suddenly he was soaring upwards, and now only a bird-like outline dotted the night sky.

The strange thing is I remember nothing else. Not the returning home or the sneaking unseen back into the house or indeed anything at all. I only know that I awoke the next morning with a dreadful fever, burning hot, as if I had suffered an illness in the night and I began to wonder whether I had seen anything at all, or if in fact I had dreamed every moment.

I told my father everything as I lay in bed. About the long shadow of Mister Tallis, about the children in the park who called his name and most of all, about the strange scene I had witnessed in the street.

And then I gave him my theory: on dragons, I mean, and on their habits for hording and hiding treasures and coins. It all made perfect sense. Or so I thought.

'You must understand that you have not been well,' began my father. 'You have suffered a high temperature brought on by a fever. Such things lead to strange visions and hallucinations,' he insisted and he put my mind at rest.

Later, I found out for sure.

When the day had grown long and I felt slightly better, but still hot, I suggested to my mother I might take a brisk walk. She was not happy about this but gave in. I did not intend to do anything other than bring myself around but unintentionally I found myself along the same route as the one I thought perhaps I'd only dreamed of.

And there upon the ground where the cold snow had frozen solid was the answer.

Deep in the crispy white were the footmarks of the long tall Mister Tallis. They went from two large boot imprints to four claw marks in a straight line until at last, right where I was sure he had taken to the sky, they disappeared altogether.

33

The Shoemaker's Apprentice

Polish Tale

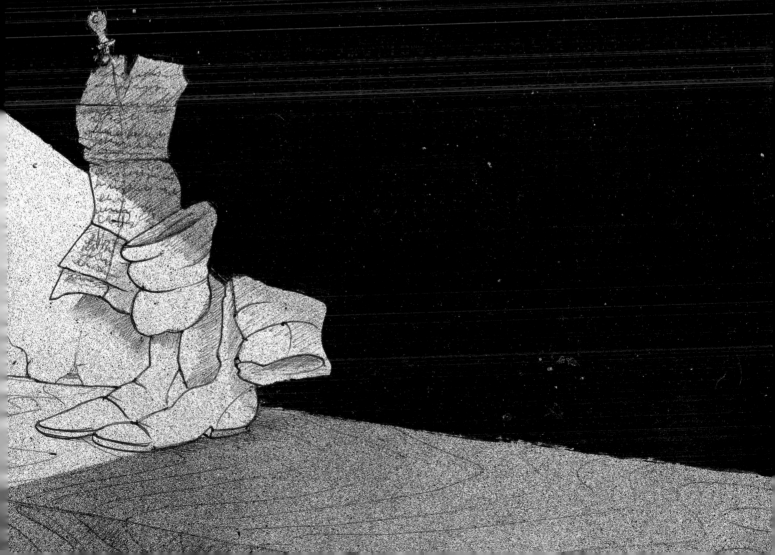

Allow me to take you to Wawel Hill. It sits on the banks of the Vistula River in the city of Krakow. At the time I take you back there it is the capital of Poland and King Krakus sits on the throne. It is a peaceful place and the people live in harmony. But it was not always that way.

Why? Well let me take you back much further in time. You wouldn't know it but we are in the same spot. There are no buildings, only farmland and Wawel Hill is just that – a simple hill.

Simple except for the fact that beneath the camouflage of the wild green grass something was stirring below. Down, deep down, beyond the wind-blown surface, through the lifeless stretch of earth to the hollow at the bottom of the hill. A great expansive cave. Not a damp and cold cave. No, a cave kept warm and dry by the fire-belching breath of a sleeping dragon.

For a hundred years he had slept. Generations of children had grown up and had had children of their own. People and families had come and gone. Through his long hidden sleep, they had told tales of the beast that came to Wawel Hill and his story had mellowed into legend until eventually the legend was forgotten.

In the coming years the village grew up around the top of the hill. The first foundation stones of the cathedral were placed in the ground and the turrets of the castle reached upwards into the blue sky which was reflected in the Vistula River. And all the while he slept.

The heart of the city was alive. People went about their business.

The market stalls were busy with buyers and sellers. And down, deep down, only the beating heart of the great beast could have assured you that he was alive.

It was late one night. A huge, lazy eye opened slowly. And then another. A great coil of a tail wound itself loose and six scaly limbs stretched themselves into life. Something had awoken. It was no longer tired, only hungry.

When something so large emerges from its lair it is hard not to notice. The ground shook beneath the buildings. Startled eyes opened in mid sleep to the rolling rumble across the countryside. Faces watched from windows as the six-legged fire breather crawled to the top of Wawel Hill. If the legend of the dragon had been forgotten, it was now well and truly awake.

It forced its way through the walls of

the village and trampled around belching fire all the while and setting alight the haystacks and the canvas tops on the market stalls. As people mistakenly came out from their homes he devoured them one by one and only when his belly was full did he return to the warmth of his lair.

And this was only the beginning. Daily he rampaged through the streets and houses of the village or tore across the nearby fields consuming the livestock that belonged to the farmers. Very quickly his hunger had turned into an all-consuming desire to swallow up everything in his path and he was soon reminded of his liking for the taste of small children.

We have all heard the tales of old: of the dragon that eats up the locals and the king who calls for a brave young knight to rescue his people. Well, I am afraid that this story does not have such an ending. Far from it. For every brave man that mounted a horse and took a sword in his hand was shaken between a thousand piercing fangs before he was barbecued and swallowed whole.

A young man named Krakus stood at the castle door and asked to see the king.

'Who are you, boy?' laughed the guards and they sneered at the holes in his clothes and his bony frame.

'I am Krakus,' he began, 'and I am only a shoemaker's apprentice, but I know I can defeat the dragon.'

Now they laughed at him even more and when the king and all his staff had heard enough they turned him away.

In the days that followed the destruction continued. Fire blazed across the thatched roofs in the night. Small buildings were trampled under foot. Villagers scattered like ants as the chase ensued. Screams echoed through the valley and as the population grew smaller the whole city grew poorer.

The king looked out through his window at the destruction. An unattended horse stood in the courtyard. The sign of another brave knight lost in the battle. His mind began to wonder and then he called for his guard.

'Bring me the shoemaker's apprentice,' he requested. And he was brought before the king to be questioned.

'How could a small boy like yourself defeat the power of such a beast?' enquired the king. 'You have no sword at your side and no shield. You've never ridden a horse and even for your profession, you're the frailest thing I ever saw.'

'I would not beat the dragon with physical force,' insisted the boy. 'No one can do that. The things you need to defeat the dragon are here among your people, on the stalls of the market that lies in tatters.'

'Very well,' said the king, who was now looking confused, 'you must go away and show me what you can do.'

And so the shoemaker's apprentice went back to the shoemaker's workshop where he readied the tools of his trade. The needle and thread would come in handy.

Then he went to the broken market stalls. All he needed was right there. First he went to the butcher, then to the grocer and finally the matchmaker. He returned with three dead rams, a batch of hot spices and a large quantity of sulphur. He laid out his ingredients on the worktop. He slit the rams' stomachs from end to end and stuffed their insides with the sulphur and the fiery hot spices. When he had done this to all three he stitched them back together with his needle and thread.

He left the shoemaker's shop and put the rams into a small cart.
He wheeled it to the bottom of the hill and left the rams at the entrance to the cave.

When the dragon emerged in hunger he saw the meal at his door and readily devoured it without so much as the blink of an eye. But the sulphur and spices burned inside him. A scorching, burning ball of heat boiled up inside his belly. Too hot, he thought. Hotter even than the flames that he hurled from the back of his throat.

He wandered painfully down to the Vistula river. He drank and drank and drank and drank but it was never enough. No matter how much he swallowed he could not dampen the fire inside him. His stomach swelled with water and his insides recoiled in pain. He drank so much that at length his stomach burst and he lay dead on the banks of the river.

And needless to say, young Krakus was not just the shoemaker's apprentice anymore. He married the king's daughter and when her father had passed on he took the throne. Around the hill a whole city grew up and in memory of their king they named it Krakow and to this very day the bones of the dragon are fixed over the door of the cathedral to remind the city that sometimes brains and wit can succeed where brute force might fail.

All in a Day's Work

By Chris Mould

Now listen, and listen carefully.

The dragon is a shy creature. He won't reveal himself to you; you must go and find him. Around these parts he will mostly dwell in the darkened depths of a cave. More than likely he will be curled around some great, glistening horde of treasure.

Why?

Well of course the dragon is always keen to protect what he believes belongs to him. These hillsides are his home and he considers that the gold that glitters in the depths of those mines is his and only his.

Simple as that!

Now you must approach him carefully. He has a nasty habit for lashing out with those huge claws of his. The front feet are the ones to watch. They will strike first. And watch those teeth, razor-sharp they are. He would think nothing of slicing you in two given half the chance.

While we're on the subject the snout is also to be avoided. What might seem like an insignificant puff of smoke can instantly flower into a scorching ball of orange flame. Very painful, I can assure you. It is best to be warned than to find out first hand.

Anyway, I am getting lost in my thoughts of fangs and fire. Never mind all that.

Once you have managed to sneak up on him, take out the glass vial from under your cloak. Get yourself underneath the folds of those wings where the skin is less leathery and take a little jab with your knife – look out for those back legs now!

Only a drop of dragon's blood is needed in your container. Get this and your task is complete.

Oh and when you get back there's a heap of washing. These floors need a scrub and the scullery is a mess, so don't be too long. At your pace it will be dark before you even get started.

Well, run along then!

What on earth are you looking so worried about?

The Eyeless Dragons

Chinese Folklore

'Something is missing,' declared the Chinese Emperor.

He was inspecting the newly constructed temple in the square. He scratched at his bearded chin and raised one eyebrow as he gazed around the large central room of the shrine.

'Dragons!' he announced and decided right there and then that the walls should be festooned with paintings of the magnificent beasts.

A polite knock at the door was the first that Yang Li knew of his task. A message had arrived from the Emperor at the palace. What could it possibly be? Yang Li was a mere artist who struggled to scratch himself a living and the Emperor was a sovereign ruler with great power.

'Allow me to explain,' said the messenger calmly as Yang Li grew nervous.

The Emperor wished for great works of art in the temple. He desired the most spectacular of oriental dragons to be placed around the walls. Only recently he had seen the work of Yang Li and with that in mind he had sent out his errand boy.

Yang Li was honoured. He'd built up a reputation for his artwork and dragons were his domain; there was no one who knew their form quite like he did.

All eyes were on the temple. By day, the people watched Yang Li come and enter the great doors and, at night, they watched him leave and return home. No one could wait to see the outcome and no one was allowed to enter while he performed his task. For many days and many nights the work went on, often into the early hours. Soon the task would be complete.

At length and with much relief the Emperor was informed that he could come and view the finished masterpiece. And what a sight it was! On each of the four walls of the palace was a tremendous work of art. The Emperor was delighted but there was something he could not understand.

'Why are the dragons without sight?' exclaimed the Emperor. 'None of them have eyes. Not one of them can see.'

'But, your honour, if I give them the power of sight, they will see that they dwell inside the darkness of your temple and the dragon is born to roam the earth,' said Yang Li.

'Nonsense,' said the Emperor. 'They are merely decorations. They do not live and breathe like you or me.'

'I'm sorry to disagree,' said Yang Li. 'But the truth is quite the opposite and if I give them the power of sight, they shall flee.'

At that moment the messenger boy came to Yang Li's side and whispered to him that he was disagreeing with the Emperor of all China. But Yang Li would not give in.

'You must paint the eyes. I insist,' stated the Emperor.

But Yang Li knew he was right. He had studied the dragon for many years. He knew its form and feared its reputation. 'You cannot play games with the dragon,' insisted Yang Li. 'He is a most unforgiving creature.'

Again the messenger boy came to his side and whispered into his ear. 'Not only are you disagreeing with him, but now you are arguing with him,' he exclaimed.

The Emperor came closer. He tightened his expression and stared at Yang Li with a piercing look. The messenger trembled and moved away.

'I shall say this only once,' the Emperor promised. 'Take your brush and paint the eyes upon the dragons. If you refuse, you will never see the light of day again.'

Yang Li looked back at the Emperor. He did not have the nerve to push it any further than he already had. With a sigh and a sorrowing heart he gave in.

'Very well,' said Yang Li. 'I will do as you wish.' He took his brush and carefully painted the eyes on to the first of the four dragons.

'There, you see,' said the Emperor. 'Now the first of your dragons is complete. Please do the same to the remaining three.'

But before Yang Li could even lift his brush again a clap of thunder resounded over the temple. Lightning struck the roof of the building and as the walls shook and the columns trembled the first dragon emerged from the wall.

Its shoulders arched upward and its head reared and turned to greet its maker. And then using its front feet to clamber away from the wall it emerged from the flat surface as brickwork and plaster crumbled around its powerful limbs.

The gathering crowd was panic stricken. Many threw themselves to the floor and others hid behind the pillars and columns. A few ran out into the street screaming their warning of a large dragon about to leave the temple.

They were followed by the winding twisting shape of the dragon as it burst into the air with the walls of the temple crashing around it.

Yang Li knew that the dragon meant no harm. He simply wished to be free and the artist watched calmly as his creation materialized. And then the whole city watched as the beast took to the sky and circled over the whole of the earth, never to return to the wall of the temple.

And the three remaining eyeless dragons?

Well of course, at the insistence of the Emperor, they remained just as they were!

The Dragon Thief

By Chris Mould

They called me the Dragon Thief. Not because I stole dragons, oh no. That would be too difficult, of course, and rather pointless.

No, rather, I stole *from* dragons. I'd seen most breeds. Some I fought with, like the Nordic Fire Breathers, others, like the Fen Dragons, I escaped from, across the southern plains.

Some I went in search of and never found. I never made it through the ice caves to the Crystal Wing and nor could I manage the great depths of the oceans that would have lead me to the black dragons of the abyss. Others, I saw but never reached. I've watched the Great Northern Fire Drifters soar over the Arctic at night as they breathed their flames to light the way. A magnificent sight, yes, but I never came any closer to them.

Often I searched for the woodland dragon. I looked high and low for his small wings and lime green scales but never found him, though I believe I was bitten once by something that resembled his kind.

Once, I speared a water dragon from my boat as I was followed and then attacked in the thick of a storm. Quite an experience I can tell you, to live in such fear out on the water, with nothing concrete to grasp hold of or hide behind.

Not every dragon is a threat of course. It is quite possible to get into a fight with one but it is also possible to watch them from a safe distance or to make peace with the right breed.

I tamed a young Snapdragon once but as it grew larger it outgrew the need for my care. It became boisterous and difficult to handle and we parted – the best decision for both of us, in the end, I'm sure.

Always, I took whatever I could.
Mostly I would seek out a cave
dweller and watch and wait for it to
settle into sleep before I spoiled
myself with the riches from his
horde. Many times I would go
back repeatedly while it slept.
Dragon sleep is quite something.
It can last for a hundred years if it
remains undisturbed. Well why not?
With a full belly and a burning fire
within and not being in any
particular rush, why on earth would
you need to wake up?

And you wouldn't want to waken
one accidentally. There is nothing
quite so frightening as a dragon awoken
from her slumber. No I don't think there is an
occupation more dangerous than stealing the
rewards of the fire breather.

But it wasn't always their possessions
I took. There were people who would pay me
for almost anything: bones or blood, scales
and toenails, that kind of thing. Used in a

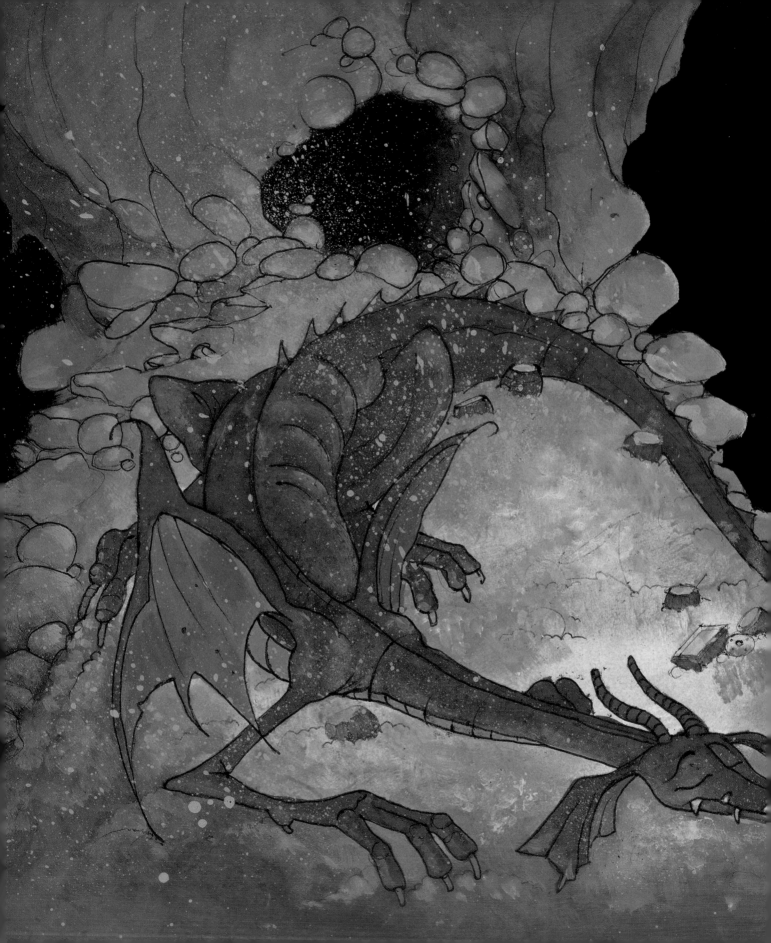

potion or spell, they were said to possess great qualities. I knew nothing of this, I only did the deed and took the money. Many of my clients were sorcerers and the like.

An old wizard I knew paid me handsomely for dragon smoke! Now what do you think of that? And you couldn't fool him. The thick black smoke from a fire or a chimney pot would never do. No, he knew dragon smoke when he saw it. Quite blue it was, he insisted. And it wasn't easy to collect either. You needed to be around a roused and angry dragon to pick up a sample of his smouldering breath, that's for sure.

And what became of me? Well I'm sure you don't wish to know but it will help pass the time, if I tell you.

I was on one of my usual hunts for treasure. I'd seen the smoke I knew to be what we called 'dragon cloud' piping upwards from the edge of a forest, a certain clue that there were dragons around. I made my way

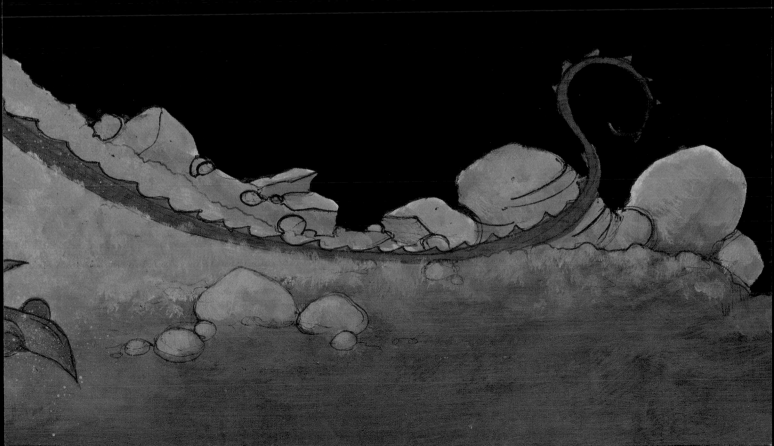

through the ferns and bracken and towering pines until I reached what I suspected would be caves.

Sure enough I was right and before too long I was finding my way through a twisting maze of curved and contorted rock. I was used to this kind of discovery and I knew that I drew close to my find.

Heat from the dragon had warmed the rock and where at first it had been cold and damp, down here it was warm to the touch. Soon I was standing in the warmth of the lair. I studied my victim closely as she lay in a silent heaving slumber. She was a fine specimen: deep red with a yellow underbelly and huge great wings that nursed her body like a blanket.

Beneath her was a shining great horde. She was curled comfortably around it with her forked tail almost touching her snout. As she slept I would soon have my hands upon it. I drew nearer and breathed carefully. Soon I felt comfortable. She rested and I took. I disappeared and came back for more. I did this more than once.

That was my mistake. I could have ended it on the second trip or even the first. I was greedy! And I'd grown too confident. I must have woken her as I searched. I was picking over the horde when I suddenly felt something. It was a great claw, a front one, pinning me down and holding me effortlessly.

And what do you suppose happened then? Well to my surprise, she bargained with me.

Oh yes, I learned to speak in dragon tongue as a young boy. She gave me a choice. I could be eaten alive there and then in cold blood or I could be released the next time she awoke.

And what do you think I chose to do?

Well yes, of course, you're right. I chose the latter. It's what anyone else would have done. It seemed like the easy option, just to wait until she next stirred. It was certainly a better deal than being devoured in seconds by gnashing teeth and burning breath. Or so I imagined.

But as I told you earlier, a dragon can sleep for a hundred years . . .

And so here I am, all these years on, still trapped beneath her claw. I haven't moved since. Even whilst I was alive I could barely shift my aching body and I certainly can't feel anything now, not anymore. So I just lie here, waiting, with my bag of gold in my hand and only my poor bones to speak of.

She should awake any time soon I would have thought.

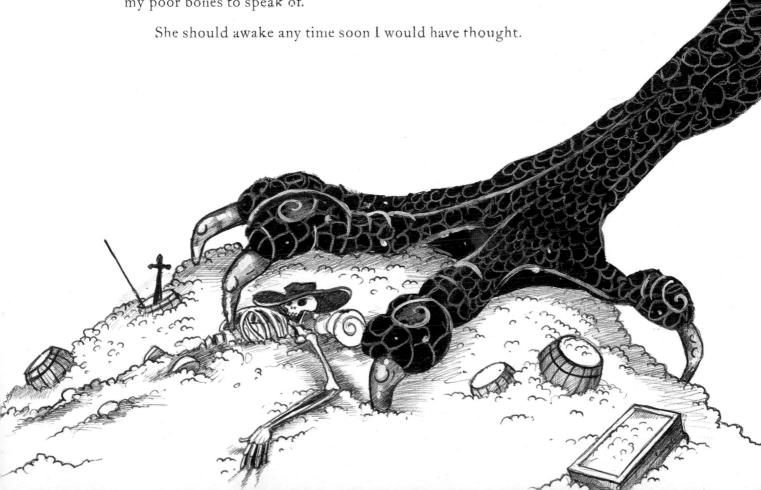

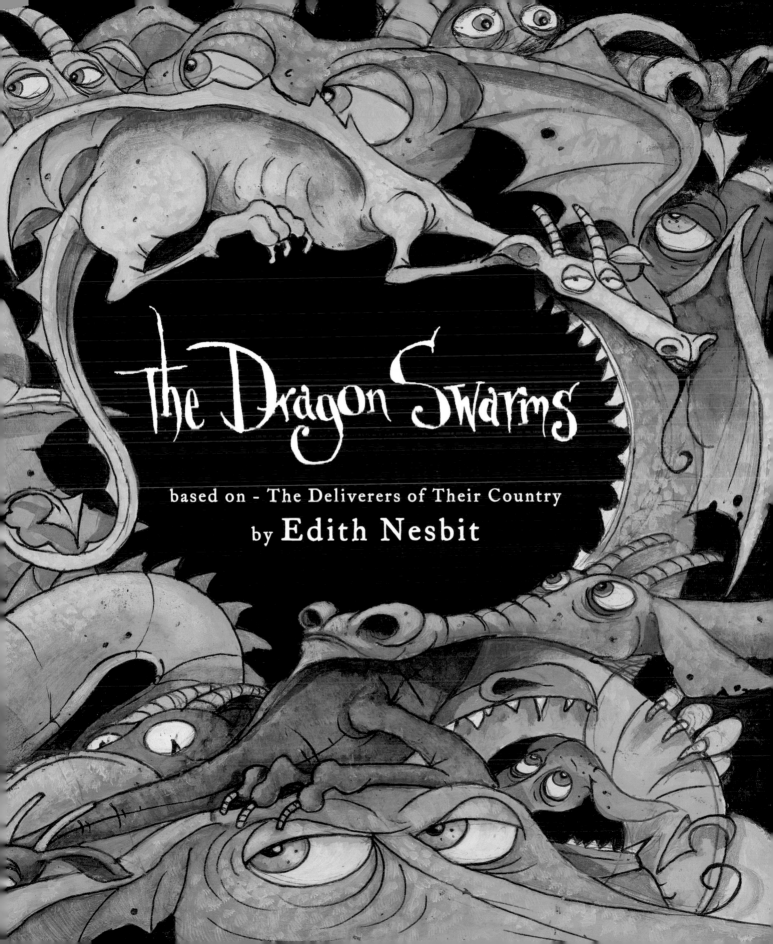

The Dragon Swarms

based on - The Deliverers of Their Country

by **Edith Nesbit**

It all began when Ellie got something in her eye. It hurt a great deal and felt like a red-hot spark, only it seemed to have legs and wings, like a fly. Her father was a doctor, so of course he knew exactly how to take things out of eyes. And then he wandered off to one side mumbling to himself about how curious it was. He placed it carefully under the microscope and continued in his chatter, announcing that he may have found some undiscovered creature.

'Mmmm . . . four limbs, and a bat-like wing. Five toes, unequal in length and a very long body.'

But at teatime the event was overshadowed by something else.

There was something in Harry's tea. Harry was Ellie's brother. At first he thought it was an earwig. He scooped it out on to his spoon and was about to squash it when it shook itself and flopped on to the tablecloth, showing two wet wings.

'It's a tiny newt!' exclaimed Harry.

But by the next morning the newt was insignificant. Cleaning his boots on the doorstep Harry suddenly dropped everything he held and screamed that he was burnt. From inside the black boot came a lizard the size of a kitten. Its large leathery wings stretched open and then it was off into the air.

'Did you see that?' shouted Ellie. 'It was a dragon. Like the one that Saint George killed.' And she was right.

That afternoon poor Towser, their dog, was bitten in the garden by a dragon about the size of a rabbit. And soon the papers were full of stories of winged lizards appearing throughout the country. Of course the papers would not call them dragons, because no one believes in dragons nowadays and they were far too sophisticated to engage in fairy stories.

At first there were only a few sightings here and there but within a matter of weeks they were everywhere. Sometimes you could see them in the air flocking like birds, until eventually there were so many they were more like swarms of bees.

They were all alike except for their differing sizes: green and scaly with four legs and huge great wings that sported a yellowy colour when the light passed through their thin membranes.

They breathed fire and smoke as all proper dragons should but the papers kept on pretending they were lizards. That was, of course, until the editor of the Standard was picked up and carried away by a particularly large one, which changed the outlook somewhat. When the largest elephant in the zoo was carried off by a dragon, the papers gave up pretending altogether and 'ALARMING PLAGUE OF DRAGONS' was the next day's headline.

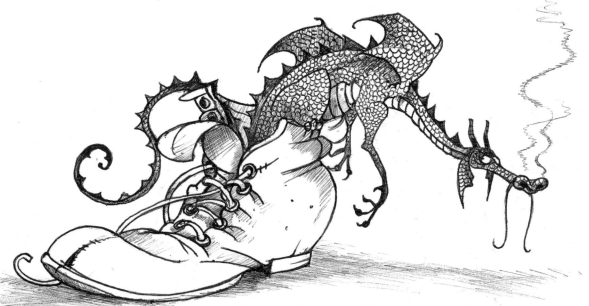

If you stayed indoors you were mostly safe from the big ones but the little ones were everywhere. The ones as big as earwigs got into the soap and the butter. The ones as big as pigeons could be found in drawers or containers and would bite the ends off your fingers when you reached in to grab something. The ones as big as dogs would curl up in the bath or at the bottom of your bed, revealing themselves when it was too late and scorching the eiderdowns and pillows. It was always a bit of a shock to find a dragon in your bed, but luckily the ones that liked the beds, didn't eat people, only lettuce!

The larger they were the more they ate. The tiniest peaceful ones lazed in the fields munching on the summer blossoms. If only the rest had been the same, but no, there was no chance of that.

The slightly bigger ones chewed on bricks and stones. The next size up from that would carry away people's pets. It became quite normal to see a neighbour's cat flying overhead or to watch a dog taking its afternoon walk, and then being snapped up by a beast in mid flight.

And as for the largest dragons. Well, their diet was the most alarming. When the locals saw the cattle being snapped up they thought they'd seen everything. But that was before they saw elephants being whipped up from the enclosures at the zoo.

As much as could be done was done, but still they came. They were killed in great numbers by many people. The shops were filled with dragon poisons and lizard-proof this and beast-proof that, yet somehow there seemed to be more dragons than ever. And after a while, Ellie and Harry were fed up with having to stay inside to avoid the dragons as big as elephants that ate boys and girls. They wanted to go outside and play in the fields, and see their friends before they all disappeared.

They'd already lost a small number. Several had been snapped up on their way out of school. Someone said it would have been kinder to take them on the way in.

Three were taken from the playground. One from the swing. It was Harry's friend, Walter. He went backwards and forwards three times. On the third attempt the swing came back down on its own and the boy was gone.

There was always one dragon perched on the roof of the sweet shop, waiting for the roundest children to come toddling out. Eventually no one went in there at all.

'What should we do?' whined Ellie.

'We ought to wake Saint George of course,' said Harry. 'He is the only person who would know how to deal with dragons.'

'But how do we do that?' she begged.

'We must go and look,' he announced. 'You shall wear a dragon-proof frock and I shall smear myself with the best dragon poison. We will go to St. George's church and we will find him there.'

And that's what they did. Ellie wrapped herself in dragon-proof muslin (there was no time to make the frock) and Harry made a smeary mess of himself with the poison (the sort that's safe for humankind and incredibly deadly to dragon types).

When they reached the church they searched the graveyard until, at last, they found the tomb of Saint George, where his marble figure lay dressed in armour upon the slab with his hands held across his chest.

They spoke to him but he did not hear. Harry shook the great marble shoulders but it was no good. Then Ellie began to cry. She threw her arms around his marble neck and kissed his cheek until a tear ran down upon the cold stone. 'Oh, dear, good, kind Saint George, please wake up and help us.'

And at that, Saint George woke up and stretched himself. 'Whatever is the matter?' he asked. But when he heard of all the dragons he shook his head.

'That's too many for poor old George,' he insisted. 'I wouldn't have a chance. But what's the weather been like lately?'

'It's been fine,' said Ellie, wondering what the weather had to do with anything, 'The hottest this country has ever seen so my father says.'

'Ahh, I thought as much,' said the champion. 'Dragons can't stand the cold and damp you see,' he explained. 'If only you could find the weather taps . . . ' And he settled back down on his slab, yawning.

'Wait,' shouted Harry. But it was not enough. Saint George was fast asleep.

'We shall never find the weather taps,' said Ellie. 'Not without some help.'

Just then, a dragon the size of an elephant swooped down and caught the children in his claws and before they had even realized what was happening, they were soaring back up into the air. Over hills and fields they flew. Far and wide they rode in the clasp of the great talons. They passed many other dragons of all shapes and sizes as they wound their way through the landscape.

On the top of a mountain the great beast stopped to rest. He had come so far that he lay down on his great green scaly side, panting and very much out of breath. As he rested Ellie and Harry sneaked out from his grasp and tiptoed towards a crack in the rocks where they stole inside a cave-like opening and hid. They were quite safe. It was way too narrow for the dragon. But he had awoken at their movements and bellowed smoke and fire at them so they ventured further in. The opening grew bigger and soon they came to a great door, which said:

UNIVERSAL TAPROOM. PRIVATE.

Well, they had to go in, private or not. The other way led them back out to the dragon. And when they went inside, they found a room full of taps all labelled neatly. They understood at once that they had reached the taps that Saint George had spoken of. From here all the weather of the world was controlled. They read the labels: South Wind, East Wind, Rain, Hail, Snow etc.

The big tap labelled sunshine was turned fully on and at the far end of the room a looking glass showed all that went on in the world outside. Baking sun blazed across the land and hordes of dragons filled the skies, swooping and soaring.

Ellie turned on the tap labelled snow. It was stiff and so Harry came to her side and turned it with her. And then they ran to the glass to see what happened. They could see the snow falling and the dragons looking up at the sky in surprise. They didn't seem to know which way to go and many were crashing into each other in panic. Others stopped to find shelter. Soon the skies were completely empty.

'It's working,' cried Ellie, and then she and Harry ran back to the taps and squeezed on the one labelled rain. It was a little rusty but they managed it in the end. Again, they watched through the glass as rain poured and the dragons began to wriggle, and then they wriggled a little less. Eventually many of them lay upon the ground and grew quite still, so the children guessed that the damp had put out the fire inside them. It was then that they turned on the hail and after a while there seemed to be no more dragons moving.

'Hooray,' said Ellie. 'All the dragons are dead!'

They'll put up a monument to us!' laughed Harry, 'for delivering our country.'

And as they watched the looking glass, one by one, the dragons were washed away, collecting and then disappearing in great green masses and scattered green shoals. When the sunshine returned there was not a single trace of dragon left. And then the children turned away from the mirror and left the cave to return home, for it was getting late and they were sure father and mother would wonder where they were.

The journey back was even longer than the journey there and when they reached home, the doctor scolded them for being away so long and sent them to bed. There was not a word of thanks for the dragons. It seemed as if everyone had forgotten them.

Except, if you looked closely round the doctor's study, you might just see the one that was in Harry's teacup and the one that was in Ellie's eye in little matchboxes on his shelf, gathering dust.

the Dragon's Teeth

Greek Mythology

Cadmus, King of Thebes awoke in the night. He tossed and turned endlessly until at last he climbed out of his bed. He stood at the window and looked out over the city.

Even now, in the early hours he sensed their coming, making their way across the dark plains, rattling their swords against their shields and thundering across the hills on their horses. When would they arrive? When would they make their move? Maybe they were only days away, or even hours. A strange light filled the sky. Cadmus was superstitious. Perhaps such colours warned of the danger ahead.

His mind raced through previous days. His people were now free of the great dragon that had guarded the spring of Ares, but at great cost. Many brave men had died in the struggle to be rid of the beast. And now, as war loomed, he was without a powerful force behind him and the great city of Thebes lay under threat. The rotting corpse of the beast lay outside the city under the baking sun and served only to remind them how many lives had already been lost. How could he possibly

gather an army at this late hour? He returned to his bed and lay there quite restless for some time.

Something stirred at his feet through the darkness. A bright light came upon him and though he thought he dreamed, he was surely awake and Athena the Goddess of war stood poised over his tangled bed. She was dressed in long robes with a helmet upon her head and the graceful shape of an owl resting on her shoulder.

'Hear these words, Cadmus, and remember them,' she began. 'Return to the place outside this city where the bones of the great dragon lie slumped in the baking sand. Remove his teeth, and take care to make sure that you claim every last one. Then you must take to the hills. With a pair of strong bulls you should plough the land, making deep furrows. Expect a healthy crop!'

At this, Cadmus was confused and he tried to interrupt but Athena motioned him to keep quiet. It was most important that he listened and soon it would become clear and he would understand.

'Take the dragon's teeth and sow them deep in the soil. Be warned, you must keep well back. When your crop grows, as it will do quickly, you must be careful to control it or it will soon get out of hand. Fear not, for what is born of the earth, is born for you.'

As she spoke her last words the owl flapped its wings and left through the window. And then she was gone. Had she really been there? He didn't dare suggest that she hadn't. He would not dream of ignoring the word of the gods and so he set about his task the next day with a fevered mind, ignoring all other duties.

As he set off outside the city to where the dragon lay he could not imagine what good could possibly come from sowing its teeth. But in any case he carried on and one by one he took each tooth from the jawbone of the great beast. His people stood and watched and although they did not like to question him, they wondered what it was that made him turn to such a task as this when the whole city was without an army.

As Cadmus ploughed the rough terrain of the rolling hills, he too wondered in confusion what could possibly come to him in the form of crops that would solve his most desperate need for strong and able men. But still he thought of the might of the gods and he carried on.

His assistants came to him and begged. 'Please, sire, we need to gather an army. This is not the time to be ploughing the fields.'

'Leave me alone,' he insisted, 'go back to your work.' And he carried on.

As dusk eased itself into the end of the day, the great bag over his shoulder and the weight of the dragon's teeth pulled on Cadmus' back. But as he sowed each one into the soil the weight lightened and he knew his task was drawing to a close.

When he had finished he remembered the words of Athena. He must stand well back. The crop would grow quickly and healthily. He did not realize just how quick.

As he stood and watched under a yellow sky, the earth turned red with a warm glow. What looked like the shoots of plants emerged from the sandy soil. But they were not shoots. And what looked like foliage grew up next to it. But it was not foliage.

Soon it grew clear. The shoots were tips of spears and the foliage was plumes of feathers on emerging head crests. The pointed spears advanced in rows. The heads grew up in the same way from underneath the helmets. Broad shoulders appeared, and then their chests, arms and legs, clad in bronzed shells. The scales of the dragon plated every inch of armour about their bodies and they lay upon the shields at their sides, glistening in the red light of the sunset.

Inch by inch their frames emerged from the warmth of the soil.
Under the growing darkness they turned and faced each other.
They wore the faces of ancient battle-scarred men. Their eyes were
burning white holes and their hands were clawed like the feet of the
dragon. Such was their ferocity that without an enemy to attack, they
turned on each other, until the whole of the harvest swarmed in battle.

They fought like packs of animals until at last only five were left.

The owl returned, resting on a nearby post, and then the voice of Athena came once more to the ears of Cadmus.

'This is your army, Cadmus. They are all you will ever need. Now go forth and reap the rewards of your harvest.'

The Smallest Dragon

By Chris Mould

I never believed anything of the fanciful tales my grandfather conjured up to amuse me. But, still I listened and enjoyed them. One night he caught me reading late into the early hours and warned me of the dangers of nursing a story for so long.

'Watch your fingers,' he said. 'You must have been holding that book for quite a while now!'

I had no idea what he meant by this until he sat down at my side and explained something. Something that I believe is the only true tale he ever told me.

'By far the biggest pest is the smallest dragon,' he began, and I must admit that I had no idea what he was going to say. 'He cannot be seen. He ventures far before he is noticed and then it is always too late. Such is the nature of this smallest of beasts.

'Of course he means no harm; he is a gentle creature. But to disturb the nest of a dragon is to ask for trouble. I'm sure you agree! You would not wish for someone to come barging through your door unannounced and start rampaging around your home.'

At this I stopped my grandfather. He was making no sense at all. He was about to warn me of the dangers of reading for too long and now he was off on a tangent about small dragons.

'Be patient,' he insisted, 'and listen.

'Now the smallest dragon insists on a diet of paper. And not just any old paper. Good strong stock is what's needed. He will munch his way through reams and reams over his lifetime, just to keep the fire burning

in his belly. And seeing as dragons don't care too much for the cold or the damp, what better place for a small dragon than curled up inside the spine of a good book that sits by the fire or a warm bedside. Books are always kept in dry places, of course, to prevent damage, and so what cosier choice of dwelling for such a creature.'

'Is that true?' I asked.

'Oh it's true all right. And I can prove it,' he assured me. 'Have you ever picked up a book with all the pages loose and hanging out and many of them missing? Of course you have, it's all too common. Have you noticed the shape of those torn pages? All jaggedy at the edges, like tiny teeth marks! All blotchy and brown – that's the scorching from the dragon's breath! And did you ever have what they call a paper cut from the page of a book? I bet you did and what could be more ridiculous than to think that a sheet of paper could cut you. Nonsense. A piece of paper couldn't cut you any more than a bundle of cotton wool but you believe it because that's what you've been told.

'Most likely what cut you was the tiny razor-sharp teeth of the smallest of dragons, lurking among the pages unseen, hiding in the gutter of the spreads and taking a crunch out of your fingers just when you least expected it.

'I heard from an old book binder that the chapter was invented to try and solve the problem. Just so you'd get yourself in and out of that book before the dragon struck. Read a chapter and put the book down, that's the idea. Seemed good in principle but all it takes is a good story that you can't put down and the first thing you notice is a sharp pain. And then a short scuttling sound announces something loitering in the pages.'

'OK,' I announced. 'I've heard enough. I'm convinced,' I said, smiling.

'Good night,' said my grandfather. 'And take heed of my warning.' He blew out my candle, took the book from my hands and placed it on the bedside table. Then he closed the door and left the room.

And I would never have thought anything else of his story, but as I lay there for a moment with my eyes open in the dark, I swear I saw a wisp of blue smoke rise from the pages of the book.

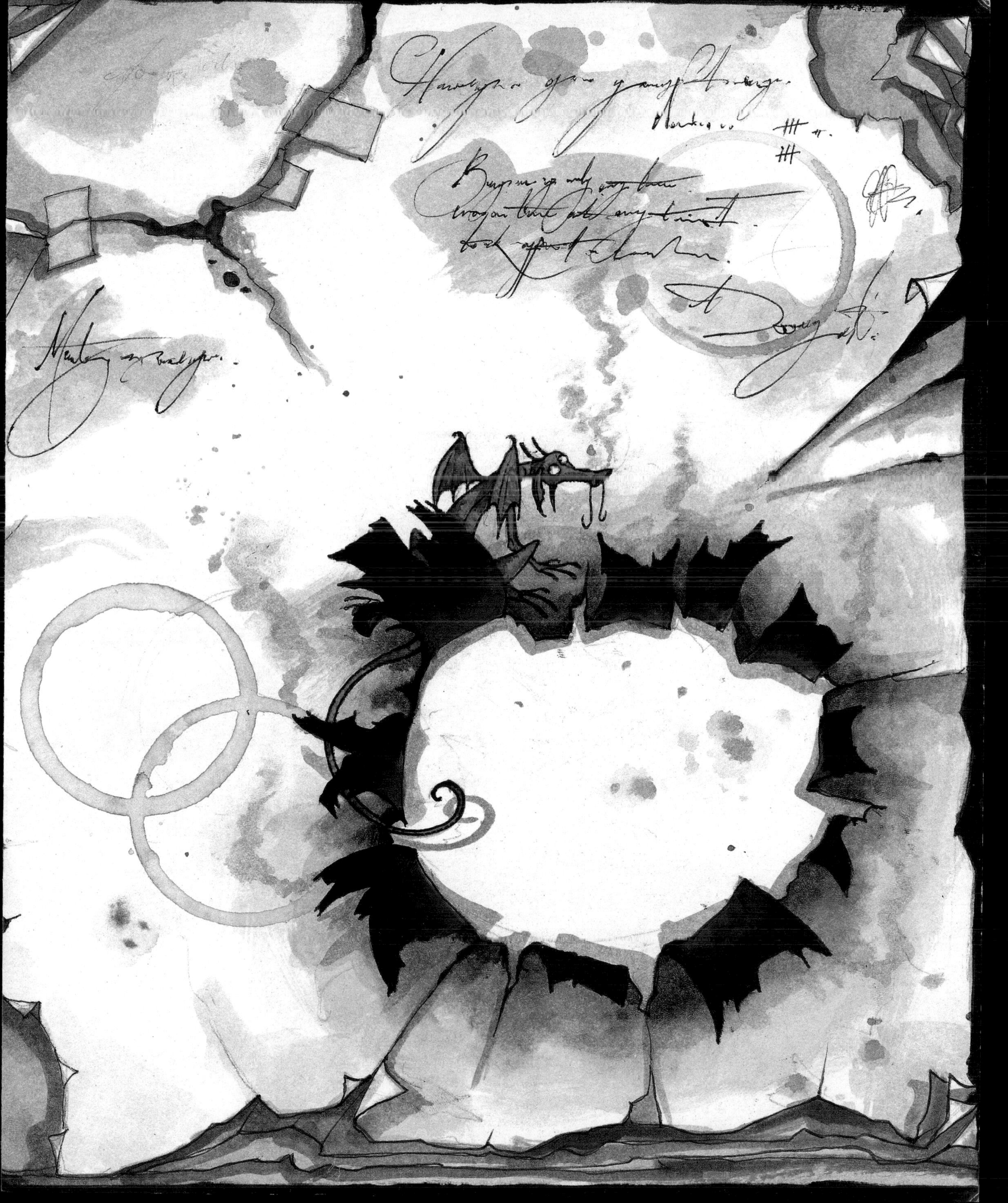

*Now you've heard
these tales my work is done.*

Only you can make up your mind.

And remember, if ever you should uncover

the beast of lore and legend, take good care.

To stumble upon a dragon,

is a rare thing indeed.